The Happy Frog

A Red Fox Book

Published by Random House Children's Books
20 Vauxhall Bridge Road, London SW1V 2SA
A division of The Random House Group Ltd
London Melbourne Sydney Auckland
Johannesburg and agencies throughout the world

Text copyright © Hiawyn Oram 1999
Illustrations copyright © Ruth Brown 1999

1 3 5 7 9 10 8 6 4 2

First published in Great Britain by Andersen Press Ltd 1999
Red Fox edition 2000

Printed in Singapore by Tien Wah Press (PTE) Ltd

THE RANDOM HOUSE GROUP Limited Reg. No. 954009
www.randomhouse.co.uk

ISBN 0 09 942308 1

The Happy Frog

Hiawyn Oram and Ruth Brown

RED
FOX

Once, there was a frog called Frances.
Frances was a happy frog.
If she wasn't hopping, she was jumping.
If she wasn't jumping, she was exploring.
One day, she came to some palace gardens.
For a while, she played hopscotch
on the paving stones.
Then, as it was a very hot day
and the ornamental pond looked cool
and inviting, she decided to take a swim.
She dived and splashed,
swam a few lengths of breaststroke,
swam a few lengths of backstroke . . .

and stretched out amongst the ferns
to soak up some shade.
"Gotcha!" came a triumphant miaow.
Frances felt the end of a sharp claw.
She felt herself being dragged up
some steps . . . and then she fainted.

When she came round she was lying between
the polished boot of a handsome young prince
and the nose of a smug-looking cat.

"Good work, Smug!" said the prince, picking
Frances up and putting her on the table.
"It's frog's legs for dinner! My favourite!"
Shaking with fear, Frances spoke out.
"Oh, please, good sir! Don't eat my legs!
They're the only ones I have and without
them how will I hop and jump?"
Now it was the turn of the prince to jump.
"A talking frog!" he cried. "I wonder
if one can eat the talking variety?"
"Oh, I do beg you not to," said Frances.
"In fact, if you will leave my legs alone,
I'll give you anything you ask for!"
"Anything I ask for?" the prince laughed.
"And what could a little frog
ever offer a tall, rich,
handsome prince?"

"A kiss, of course, Henry, don't you know *anything?*"
cried the queen, sweeping into the room.
"When a handsome prince kisses any old frog,
she turns into a beautiful princess
which is the one thing we're looking for.
Well . . . go on . . . I'm waiting!"
Frances did her best
to hop out of kissing range.
The prince made a million excuses
but in the end the queen got her way . . .

and with Smug's help and just one kiss,
Frances was turned into a beautiful princess!
The prince was very pleased. "Mother!"
he cried. "You're a genius!"
"No, I've just read my fairy tales,"
said the queen. "Now, let's look at you,
child . . . Yes, you will do very well!
Dinner's at eight. I'll see you there."

Now, somehow, Frances
got to that dinner on time.
But she cried all through it.
She cried through the first
course. She cried through
the second course
and she cried all night
in her palatial bed.
The prince tip-toed in
to ask what the matter was.
"I don't *feel* like a princess," she wept.
"Well, you certainly look like one,"
said the prince. "And a very beautiful one
at that. Now *please* dry your eyes
and try to be the part."

So Frances dried her tears
– what else could she do? –
and did her best to play the part.
The wedding was arranged.
The wedding bells rang out.
The world was at her feet.
"What a beautiful girl!"
the crowds cheered.
"How lucky we are
to have our great prince
married to such a princess!"

And that might have been
the end of that except that it wasn't.
One night, the royal cook
served frogs' legs.
As the lid came off the dish,
Frances screamed and screamed
and screamed!

She ran out of the palace,

through the gardens,

through the night,

through the forest and back
to the well where she was born.

There she sat and sobbed until Frank
– a frog who never went far from the well –
could bear it no longer.
"Why such distress, sweet princess?"
"Because," wept Frances, "it's all wrong.
I'm not a princess. I'm not, I'm not."
"Would a kiss help, d'you think?"
said Frank. "They often do."
"But what if it just turns you
into a prince?" sniffed Frances.
"A risk I'm ready to take," said Frank.
Then up he hopped and kissed her,
with a kiss so enchanted
it turned Frances back . . .
from an unhappy princess
into a happy frog.

Their wedding was not long afterwards.
And all I can say is, I was there . . .
and what a wedding *that* was!

Some bestselling Red Fox picture books

THE BIG ALFIE AND ANNIE ROSE STORYBOOK
by Shirley Hughes
OLD BEAR
by Jane Hissey
OI! GET OFF OUR TRAIN
by John Burningham
DON'T DO THAT!
by Tony Ross
NOT NOW, BERNARD
by David McKee
ALL JOIN IN
by Quentin Blake
THE WHALES' SONG
by Gary Blythe and Dyan Sheldon
JESUS' CHRISTMAS PARTY
by Nicholas Allan
THE PATCHWORK CAT
by Nicola Bayley and William Mayne
WILLY AND HUGH
by Anthony Browne
THE WINTER HEDGEHOG
by Ann and Reg Cartwright
A DARK, DARK TALE
by Ruth Brown
HARRY, THE DIRTY DOG
by Gene Zion and Margaret Bloy Graham
DR XARGLE'S BOOK OF EARTHLETS
by Jeanne Willis and Tony Ross
WHERE'S THE BABY?
by Pat Hutchins